For Mister Boy and his Big Night — J.C.S.
For Gilles and his new baby sister — S.D.

First published in 2004 by Macmillan Children's Books
A division of Macmillan Publishers Limited
20 New Wharf Road, London N1 9RR
Basingstoke and Oxford
Associated companies throughout the world
www.panmacmillan.com

ISBN 0 333 98670 9

Text copyright © 2004 Jonathan Shipton
Illustrations copyright © 2004 Suzanne Diederen
Moral rights asserted.

1 3 5 7 9 8 6 4 2

A CIP catalogue record for this book is available from the British Library.

Printed in Begium by Proost

Lucky Duck

Written by
Jonathan Shipton

Illustrated by
Suzanne Diederen

MACMILLAN CHILDREN'S BOOKS

When Lenny was a very little boy, his dad bought him a really special toy duck.

Duck was Lenny's best thing and
whatever Lenny did, Duck did too.

They played together.

They read together.

Even when Lenny went to nursery, Duck had his own special place to sit.

So, when they went to the seaside
to visit Gran, Lenny made sure
there was an extra bucket and
spade for Duck.

Lenny really liked playing
on the beach. So did Duck.

Sometimes they paddled together,
and sometimes they built
sandcastles with flags on top.

But one day, when it was time
to go home, somewhere in the rush
of packing and kissing goodbye,
Lenny's little duck
got lost.

When Lenny realised, well,
he had never been so
unhappy in his
whole life.

They searched the house, upside down and inside out.

They even looked
all along the beach,
but they couldn't find
Duck anywhere.

Poor Lenny had
to go all the way
home without his
duck to cuddle.

Lenny tried hard to be brave,
but he missed his duck very much.
Even though he had lots of other
lovely toys, no one was
quite as special as Duck.

Every night for a
long time, Duck would
appear in Lenny's dreams.
And Lenny would wonder
where Duck was and
what he was doing.

But time passed, and Lenny
grew up. He began to
play with lots of
different toys.

And he nearly forgot about the
little duck with an orange beak
and bright button eyes.

Nearly . . . but not quite.

Many years later, when Lenny was a grown-up,
he had a little boy of his own, called Ben.

One summer, Lenny took Ben to visit Gran at the seaside.

It was cold and raining, and Ben was very bored.

So Lenny said, "When I was little, I always loved exploring. Why don't you see what you can find?"

Ben crawled inside Gran's old wardrobes.

He looked underneath all the beds.

Then he found some little stairs, and climbed all the way up to the attic . . .

When Ben came
back down, he just
couldn't stop smiling.

He was holding something white and fluffy.
He held it out to show Lenny.

It was
DUCK!

His orange beak was a little
bit dirty and his white fur
was very dusty, but he was still
the same soft, cuddly Duck.

And that's what
happens with some
lucky ducks.

They get lost . . .

and squashed . . .

and left behind,
but one day . . .

. . . they find their boy!